WHEN ZOMBIES INVADE

D.E. DALY

An imprint of Enslow Publishing

WEST **44** BOOKS™

THE Z TEAM

WHEN ZOMBIES INVADE   GHOST TOWN
KIDNAPPED BY VAMPIRES   WEREWOLVES ON THE LOOSE!

Please visit our website, www.west44books.com. For a free color catalog of all our high-quality books, call toll free 1-800-542-2595 or fax 1-877-542-2596.

Cataloging-in-Publication Data

Names: Daly, D.E.
Title: When zombies invade / D.E. Daly.
Description: New York : West 44, 2019. | Series: The Z team
Identifiers: ISBN 9781538381878 (pbk.) | ISBN 9781538381885 (library bound) | ISBN 9781538382943 (ebook)
Subjects: LCSH: Zombies--Juvenile fiction. | Trains--Juvenile fiction.
Classification: LCC PZ7.D359 Wh 2019 | DDC [E]--dc23

First Edition

Published in 2019 by
Enslow Publishing LLC
101 West 23rd Street, Suite #240
New York, NY 10011

Copyright © 2019 Enslow Publishing LLC

Editor: Theresa Emminizer
Designer: Sam DeMartin

Printed in the United States of America

CPSIA compliance information: Batch #CS18W44: For further information contact
Enslow Publishing LLC, New York, New York at 1-800-542-2595.

THE **Z** TEAM

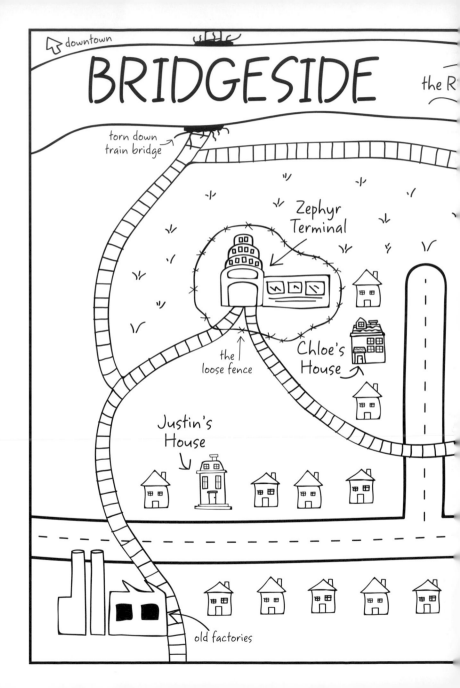

CHAPTER ONE
The Train That Couldn't Be

Trains didn't come to Bridgeside anymore. They'd stopped running years ago. Before the last factory even closed. Years before Justin was born.

But a train whistle woke Justin. Right after midnight.

He ran to his window. Once he opened it, he heard wheels chugging, too. No train lights, though. No movement below.

Justin could barely see the tracks behind his house in the dark. But he knew they were broken. Grass covered them.

No real train could get down those tracks. But it sure sounded real. And close.

The sound slowly got quieter. It seemed to be going toward the giant old train station. Zephyr Terminal. Justin had always been curious about the name. Zephyr. Zeh-fur. It meant a gentle breeze. But there was nothing gentle or breezy about this station.

The terminal had been a big deal when Justin's dad was a kid. Now it was just Bridgeside's biggest empty building. Teenagers threw rocks at its tall windows.

Justin grabbed for his phone. He opened a group message: Zephyr Team Project.

Justin took a deep breath. As the train sound faded, he texted Malik and Chloe:

> I just heard a train go by. Ghost train?

Right away, he was sorry he sent it. It was after midnight. He felt so dumb. They might not reply till morning.

Or at all.

Malik and Chloe were his closest school friends. But in summer, Malik mostly hung out with his cousins. Chloe was mostly with girl friends.

Justin spent half the summer at his mom's new apartment. Downtown. He had his brother,

Charlie. Mostly he wished he didn't have Charlie.

Malik replied with just question marks. Justin felt worse.

Chloe replied in all caps.

> **BLINKING GREEN LIGHT! FROM ZEPHYR TERMINAL!**
>
> CS

Justin leaned on his window to look. He couldn't see the building from here. But Chloe did live right there.

> **Pictures??**
>
> MB

> **TOO FAST! IT STOPPED!**
>
> CS

Justin leaned on his window screen too hard. The metal screeched. He still couldn't see—

Something banged on his wall. Justin jumped.

"Hey, king of the nerds. Whatever you're doing—cut it out!" his brother Charlie yelled.

Justin didn't want to yell. He went to his bedroom door, stepped out, and stuck his head into Charlie's room.

"Did you hear a train?"

"So?" Charlie said.

Charlie was thirteen. Two years older. It felt to Justin like he was two times as tall and broad. Charlie put pictures of motorcycles on his wall this summer. And he'd gotten a lighter, somewhere. He kept it on his nightstand. Justin hated it.

"Just—did you?"

"Don't care," Charlie said. "Get out." As Justin left, Charlie added, "If I did—it was probably just sounds across the lake. Or a truck from the highway."

Justin hadn't heard many trains in his life. But that wasn't a truck.

"Don't go thinking it's your dumb ghost stuff. You listen to too many podcasts," Charlie said. "Nerd."

"That's me," Justin muttered. He'd missed a few texts.

HEY! BLINKING. GREEN. LIGHT. Don't you remember what that means?

CS

Justin remembered. He'd been the one to write it on their

4

project poster board.

Back when Zephyr Terminal had trains, the clock in the middle of the station had a green light on it. Like the light on top of a police car.

If it blinked green, that was a warning. It told regular people, normal workers, to clear out. It meant a train was coming. Full of prisoners or coffins. A train people might not want to be around.

A bad train.

Justin took a deep breath and sent:

We could check it out tomorrow?

As they made plans, Justin heard a screech. Maybe an owl.

Or train brakes.

CHAPTER TWO
Packed for Adventure

The blinking green light hadn't scared Chloe. It lit up the broken windows of Zephyr Terminal. Made them look like a monster's teeth. It was so quick she'd almost missed it.

Chloe was glad she hadn't. She'd been preparing for this moment most of her life.

She watched a lot of spooky TV shows with her older sisters.

First thing in the morning, she packed a backpack. Flashlight, extra batteries, rabbit's foot, dreamcatcher, salt. Anything that worked against creepy things. They'd agreed to meet at noon. Chloe started waiting on her porch early.

Justin hustled up on his bike, right on time. He was out of breath.

"Worried we'd leave without you?" Chloe said, kidding.

Justin shrugged, cheeks red.

"Leave?" Malik's voice said. From the other side of the porch. He must have cut through a yard. His WowNow action-capturing camera was on his head. He climbed over the railing instead of just coming to the porch stairs.

"Where are we going?" Malik asked. "Zephyr Terminal has a fence. It's pretty high to hop."

Chloe picked up her backpack. "We're not going to hop it," she said.

Chloe led the way. They cut through neighbors' yards until they reached the fence. Here all the train tracks stopped. At Zephyr Terminal, along the river.

Chloe went to a part of fence that was loose

at the bottom. She knew she could lift it up.

"My sisters cut through here sometimes," she explained. The boys stared. "Come on!"

They ducked under, one at a time, and walked up to the terminal. It was all brick walls, sealed-up train entrances, and closed doors. The windows were way over their heads.

"We'd have to go inside to see anything," Justin said.

"Yup," Chloe said.

"We can't," Justin said.

"Don't say 'can't' until after you try," Chloe said.

"Your sisters tell you that, too?" Malik teased. "Let's try the doors. If we can't get in—"

"We go back?" Justin said.

"This was your idea!" Chloe said. She nudged Justin. "What if…it really is a 'bad train'? Shouldn't somebody check?"

"If we find a door that opens," Justin said, swallowing, "we'll check."

But the first door stayed locked. So did the second, the third…and the sixth. Malik tugged a bunch, and Chloe tried more.

Justin hadn't tried any.

"You have to try one, too," Chloe told Justin. "Team project, right?"

She hoped this wasn't the last door. Justin didn't look like he was going to tug very hard.

But the door pulled open so easily Justin stumbled backwards. Luckily, Chloe and Malik were right behind him. They kept him from falling.

Chloe leaned forward. She tried to see around Justin. Malik switched the light of his WowNow camera on.

"Here goes nothing," Malik said, charging ahead.

He beat Chloe inside—but she was right behind.

CHAPTER THREE
The Dispatch Room

Zephyr Terminal looked like an old-time movie set. Malik knew. He watched enough old movies.

Their end-of-the-year school project had taught him a lot about Zephyr Terminal. Including that it wasn't spelled "Zeffer," like it sounded. He'd printed out pictures of it for their poster board. He recognized the high ceiling. The long floor. The clock standing alone in this open space.

The movie-set part was the empty booths and counters. The signs everywhere: TICKETS, BAGGAGE, INFORMATION, NEWSPAPERS. By the stairs: TO OFFICES. Above a huge, shadowy tunnel: TO TRAINS.

Malik aimed his WowNow at the light on top of the clock.

"That's what glows green, right?"

"The warning light," Justin said.

They stood around it, waiting. Malik pulled out his phone. His fully charged battery had dropped to nothing. Weird. His WowNow had power, but not much.

Finally, Malik pointed at the TO OFFICES sign, by the stairs.

"Maybe there's a light switch," he said.

The steps were marble at first. Then old wood stairs. They stepped carefully, reaching an upstairs hallway of open offices.

There was one closed door alone at the hall's end.

It swung open when Chloe pushed. Inside was a circular desk and thick metal chair. The entire desktop was a rusty board of buttons. Nearby stood a wide board with squiggly lines.

"The dispatch room," Justin said.

"Dispatch?" Malik said.

"The guy who controlled the train routes—he'd sit here."

"Who says it was a guy—" Chloe started. She cut herself off with a gasp.

One of the squiggly route lines on the board lit up. Little lights moved toward the big circle in the board's center. Then the line went dark.

"Look," Justin said, jabbing his finger at the board. "The circle would be Zephyr. The lines were the train routes. This must show the trains arriving."

The light repeated, stopping right before the circle. Blocked.

"Train trying to come in," Justin whispered. "Over and over."

"Or something's wrong with the lights," Malik pointed out. "Don't you think that's what people would say?"

"It's what my brother would say," Justin said. He tapped the board. "I think the train's stopping where the track switched."

Malik thought of movies. Ones where trains got sent in the right direction at the last second. With the change of a lever.

"This board controls that?"

Chloe sat down in the dispatch chair. She

pressed a random button. Malik pressed a switch, too. It didn't even click.

"These wouldn't really do anything anymore," Justin said.

The board lit up again. This time, Malik thought he heard a faint train whistle.

"You try," Malik told Justin. He moved back so his camera light shone on the switches. Chloe leaned forward.

Justin looked between the rusty buttons and the board. He went for the dial by itself in the left corner. He turned it. It clicked.

On the board, the lit-up line switched direction. It reached the center.

A train whistle blew. A chugging sound was close and clear. Train brakes squealed. Right below them.

Without meaning to, Malik grabbed Justin and Chloe's arms.

A radio, nearby, crackled. A woman's voice came out: "You're through, Z Train. Follow my command. Take Bridgeside."

"Take it…where?" Chloe said. The radio crackled off.

"I don't think she was talking to us," Justin said.

From below came a grinding sound. Like train doors opening, for the first time in ages. Dragging footsteps followed.

"I don't think ghosts have footsteps," Malik said.

Slobbery moans drifted from below.

"If it's not a ghost train—" Chloe said.

Malik thought of horror movies he'd seen. "Maybe we should—"

Chloe was on her feet. Justin, already at the door. All before Malik finished saying "Run!"

CHAPTER FOUR
He's a Zombie

Justin had made a mistake with the dial. He'd wanted, badly, to prove one story true. He hadn't been thinking about the warning. Something bad was now arriving.

They hurried back down the stairs.

At the bottom, they stopped still. There was a *dead man* walking by.

He wore ragged overalls and a railroad cap. His right arm hung limp, partly pulled off. His saggy skin was green-gray.

"Don't scream," Justin whispered.

Malik stepped back one stair. "Thaaaat

better not be what I'm thinking," he said, stepping backwards again.

Justin stepped back, too. Chloe just unzipped her backpack.

The man turned toward them. Under his cap, his eyes looked both milky and bloodshot. A sharp cheekbone stuck out of his skin.

"*Zombie*," Justin whispered.

The zombie opened its mouth and shrieked. The distant footsteps suddenly stopped. Then restarted.

A flashlight from Chloe's backpack fell and rolled. She rezipped the backpack while holding some container she'd taken out.

Malik was trying to record the zombie.

"I hope they can't run," Malik said. "In some movies—"

The zombie came after them. One step, then another. Not moving too fast. Not as slow as Justin would like.

Chloe busted open the top of her container. She started shaking it everywhere. Salt. She threw salt on the stairs.

"What are you doing?" Malik said. "Let's

go—"

"I'm going," Chloe shouted. She ran up after them. Justin paused to watch. The zombie's shrieks got louder as it hit the salt. It stepped backwards—

And slipped on Chloe's flashlight. It fell onto its back. Kicking, clawing at the air.

"Justin!" Malik shouted, already upstairs.

Justin hurried to catch up. He found his friends looking out an office window. It looked down into the terminal.

Out from under the "TO TRAINS" sign— came a line of zombies. Staggering. Wearing torn old clothes and hats.

Zephyr Terminal was crowded again.

CHAPTER FIVE
Fight or Flight

They quickly found another set of stairs. Another door. And they escaped to daylight.

"How'd you know salt would work?" Justin asked Chloe.

"I didn't. I brought it for ghosts," Chloe said. They backed away from the building. "The characters use it on *Ghostfighters*. And in one episode of *Sunny the Monster Masher*."

Justin shook his head. "Those aren't real. Did this…really…?"

"Got it on film," Malik said. He took his WowNow off his head, checking it.

Justin rubbed his hair. "Do you think they

can go out in sunlight?"

A zombie shrieked, inside. Loud moans followed.

"Let's not find out!" Malik said.

"My house," Chloe said. They ran for it.

By the time they rushed into Chloe's kitchen, they were sweaty. Chloe's dark curls stuck to her forehead.

Chloe's teenage sister Em was on her laptop in the kitchen.

Chloe set the salt down and said, "Zombies. Inside Zephyr Terminal."

"You went *inside* Zephyr Terminal?" Em said. "*Not* okay—"

"Really not," Malik said. He took off his WowNow. "But look, we can show you!"

He plugged the camera into Em's laptop and opened up the new video. He fast-forwarded their walk into the Terminal, up to the clock. Up the stairs. Into the dispatch—

Right there, the video file turned to total static.

"Are you kidding?" Malik said.

They'd recorded no proof.

"Chloe!" Em said. "That's an abandoned building. There could be weird people there."

"Yes! Zombies!"

"Oh, please!" Em threw up her hands. "Seriously! You'll be lucky if I don't tell Mom!"

"Em!" Chloe said, as her sister walked off. Em had left her laptop. Justin sat down and started searching.

"We have to get someone to listen," Malik said. "Our parents. Mine are at work, but—"

"If Chloe's sister won't listen," Justin said, "you think our parents will? The police? Everybody knows we like ghost stories, vampire TV shows, monster movies—nobody's going to listen to us telling stories. We're eleven."

"I'm pretty much twelve," Malik said.

"In December! It's August!" Chloe said.

"Look—" Justin interrupted, before they argued. He showed them the results he'd pulled up on the laptop. Comments on how supernatural stuff drained phone batteries. A preview for a book called *Real Zombies* mentioned salt having powers.

"If these were true—maybe there's more that will help us, when we go back."

"Back?" Malik said.

"We need proof," Justin said.

"If my camera had just worked—" Malik said.

"It didn't," Chloe said. "Justin's right. We need to arm ourselves."

"With knowledge?" Malik said.

"And weapons," Chloe said.

"What weapons? *You're eleven*."

Chloe pointed to the salt. "This. Shovels? Baseball bats?"

"None of us play baseball," Malik said.

"Fire, maybe," Chloe said. "We don't have a lighter here...maybe some matches..."

"My brother Charlie has a lighter," Justin said.

"Good," Chloe said.

"Not good!" Malik said. "We should tell somebody, everybody—it's not our fault if they don't believe us!"

"But we switched the track," Justin said.

"The warning light was on before we got there," Malik said. "The train was already coming—"

"But not getting through," Justin said. "We did something. We—"

"Switched the track," Chloe said, at the same time as Justin.

"Fine," Malik said. He picked up the salt. "But I get to carry this."

CHAPTER SIX
Zombie Delivery

They biked to each of their houses. Malik borrowed one of Chloe's sisters' bikes. At least it wasn't pink. The jump ropes—which they packed as supplies—were all pink.

At Malik's, they found only plastic snow shovels. They took his mom's metal garden trowels. At Justin's, Malik and Chloe filled plastic baggies with salt. Justin snuck into his brother's room.

Justin's house had sharp kitchen knives. But his brother walked in when they tried taking those.

"No way," Charlie told them. "Nope, no knives. You weirdos."

"But—there's zombies," Chloe said. Justin

tried to shush her.

Charlie laughed. "What's this nerd game?"

"Nothing—we're leaving." Justin kept his brother's lighter behind his back.

Back at the terminal, they left their bikes against the fence. They snuck back under.

Malik had salt bags ready in both hands. Justin and Chloe held the jump ropes.

They went around the back of the terminal to the train entrance. That tunnel had been closed up. It was open now. But too shadowy inside to see anything.

They crouched low by the side of the building. One zombie walked out.

"Wait," Chloe whispered. "Isn't that—"

Out of the tunnel came the local delivery guy. He was in his usual brown uniform and hat. Malik couldn't imagine what he'd be delivering here.

Up close, the delivery guy's eyes were really, really bloodshot. He walked by them, moving jerkily.

"Not good," Malik whispered.

"That guy's delivered packages for years.

He was normal!" Chloe said.

"He *was*," Justin said. "*They're making more zombies.*"

"Let's do this then. We salt the next zombie to come out," Chloe said.

They waited what felt like ages. The next zombie to lurch out looked like an old-fashioned hobo. His floppy hat and coat were in tatters. His skin looked like a gray crayon wrapper, pulled tight over his bones.

Malik waited until the zombie got close. Then he threw the plastic baggies of salt at the zombie.

Both hit. Some salt struck its face. The rest rained onto its chest.

The zombie staggered as if burned, moaning. No shrieking yet. Justin and Chloe looped all the jump ropes around the zombie, tight.

They all grabbed jump rope handles and pulled the zombie through the grass. The zombie's hands were pinned under the rope, not tied. It kept reaching.

They neared the gap under the fence. Looking back, Malik saw another zombie wander out of the tunnel. Their zombie was still quiet.

"Maybe this one doesn't shriek," Malik said. To the zombie, he said, "Can you speak?"

"Zombies don't speak," Chloe said.

"Sssssss," the zombie said.

They nearly let go of the jump rope. Only their grip held it tight. That loosened the zombie's hands. It grabbed the railroad track. They tugged. But it held on.

Malik let go. Chloe and Justin kept holding the rope. Malik got out his mom's garden trowel. He used it to try to pry up the zombie's hands.

"What do you want?" Malik asked it.

"Ssss," the zombie said.

"What's your name? Who sent you?" No answer.

"Who controls you?" Justin tried.

That made the zombie answer, "Witchhhhh."

Chloe dropped the jump rope. Malik tried to use the garden trowel to keep the zombie down.

Malik looked over. "Why'd you—"

The deliveryman zombie stood on the other side of the fence blocking their escape. Ten dead-looking zombies were with him. Plus their regular neighborhood postwoman, her eyes bloodshot.

Behind him, Malik heard a chugging sound. He turned. Coming out of the tunnel was the *train*. Slowly, missing wheels, its front dented in. Zombies stood on its freight cars, hung off its doors. It chugged right toward them as if the track wasn't broken.

Malik reached to grab more salt from the backpack.

He'd forgotten the zombie on the ground. It lunged. Malik moved his hand away fast. But the zombie's rotting teeth scraped his hand. Just a scrape—but it broke skin.

Trying to stay brave, he threw salt bags to Chloe. She opened them, tossing so much salt it looked like snowfall.

Justin reached into his pocket and pulled out the lighter. He flicked the flame on.

"Get back!" he said.

The zombie on the ground crawled away. Still tangled in pink rope. The ones behind the fence stayed back. The zombie driver even stopped the train.

The deliveryman and postwoman zombies, though, kept walking. Their bloodshot eyes fixed on the flame. They moved a lot faster than the dead-looking zombies.

Justin edged left. "Follow me," he said.

"The river's that way," Chloe said. "Oh. Maybe they can't swim!"

They backed up to the water. The deliveryman and postwoman had almost reached them. They moaned like the other zombies.

Something went, "Ribbit."

All moans from the zombies around them stopped, completely.

A frog hopped over Malik's foot.

Justin looked between the frozen zombies, the frog, and the lighter he was holding.

"Get the frog!" he shouted.

Malik snagged it. The frog wriggled, slimy, in his hand. He held it up, *Lion King* style.

The zombies completely freaked out. The ones on the train crawled right back inside or under it.

The deliveryman zombie and postwoman turned away. The zombies on the other side of the fence plowed right through the wire. They slammed until the fence broke in. Then they staggered to the train.

Justin and Chloe relaxed. Malik didn't. When they looked at the hand he held the frog in, they saw why.

"It's not bleeding," Malik said. He tried not to think of what zombie bites did, in most zombie movies.

"We'll figure it out," Justin said. His voice shook. "Let's go—"

"I can't believe you took my lighter, nerd boy!" Justin's brother shouted, pedaling up on a bike. "You're so dead."

Charlie hopped off, throwing his bike down. And then he noticed the fence was down. He saw the train. But all the zombies on it were hidden.

Malik held tight to his new friend, the frog. Not good, he thought.

CHAPTER SEVEN
Not Like the Movies

"Charlie," Justin said, "You've got to listen—"

"I don't 'got' to do anything," Charlie said. He gave Malik's frog a weird look. Then he focused on the train. "How'd this get here?"

He walked closer to the train. To an open freight car.

"Charlie, please—" Justin said. His heart pounded. Charlie was a jerk. More of a jerk now that he was thirteen. And since their mom moved out. He was still Justin's only brother.

"Always wanted to jump a train," Charlie said. He eyed the distance from the ground.

"You idiot!" Chloe said, "there's zombies—"

"Don't call me an idiot," Charlie said. And then he jumped.

They all shouted no. Justin was the loudest.

Charlie grinned down from the train car.

"Losers," Charlie said.

A pile of zombies wearing hats and overalls rose from behind him. They grabbed Charlie's arms. Pulled him all the way in. The freight car door slid shut.

Justin raced forward. A few zombies crawled out from under the train. Malik aimed the frog at them. They crawled back.

"Justin, I'm sorry—" Chloe said.

"We can't leave him—"

The zombie train started reversing. Back into its tunnel. With Charlie on board.

"We don't have a way to get him out," Chloe said. "It'll be night soon. And Malik's been bitten."

"Only a little," Malik said.

"We'll come back," Chloe said. "With help. Something."

Justin nodded. He felt like he should cry—his eyes felt hot—but no tears came.

They grabbed the bikes. Charlie's bike

stayed behind. Alone.

Back at Chloe's, Justin sat at the computer. He was looking up "zombie bite cures." Malik ran hot water on his hand. Salt water, too.

Chloe tried to convince her sisters that zombies had Charlie.

Justin couldn't tell El and Em apart. Which made him remember how alike he and Charlie looked years ago. Not so much anymore.

"You okay?" Malik asked.

"I should be asking you that," Justin said.

"I feel okay," Malik said, looking down at his hand.

Malik's pocket ribbitted. "Need to find a better place for this guy," he added. "Since when are zombies afraid of frogs?"

Good point. Justin searched "zombies afraid of frogs." He found a website for a zombie museum. No, a voodoo museum. About zombies created by magic.

"Maybe these zombies aren't like your movies," Justin said. There was nothing about zombies wanting to eat brains here. Just a gross legend that brains were used to create zombies.

And other "zombie recipes." For powders. Potions.
Not just to control the dead. To turn the living
into zombies. "Maybe it's not a bite that creates
zombies."

"Yeah?" Malik said. He looked over Justin's
shoulder as Justin searched "witch + zombie +
train." He got a result.

"What's a 'witch train'?" Malik asked.

"Trains that look normal," Justin read. "But
all the workers are actually zombies. Controlled by
a witch. Anyone who jumped on
board got turned into a zombie."

"With potions. Not bites."
Malik looked down at his hand.
"I'm not going to die!"

"Right," Justin said.
"Because zombies are…"

Dead.

Chloe leaned back into the room. "El and
Em will drive us to your house, Justin. We'll tell
your dad—"

"Charlie's probably home by now," one
sister said. "I'm sure it's a prank. But if you want
to drive by the terminal—"

"No," Chloe said. She looked scared at the thought of bringing her sisters there.

Em and El rolled their eyes at each other.

The whole drive home, Justin gripped the lighter. It was off, but he hadn't let it go.

When they pulled into his driveway—

Charlie's bike *was* out front.

Justin scrambled to get out of the car. He almost squished the frog.

Inside, his dad was setting out dinner.

"Is Charlie home?" Justin said. He didn't wait for an answer. He raced upstairs.

Behind him, Chloe said, "Hi, Mr. Gill..."

Justin found Charlie's door wide open.

Charlie sat stiffly on his bed. He stared at his hands.

"Charlie, are you coming to dinner? Justin brought friends!" their dad called.

Charlie looked up. His eyes were bloodshot.

"Don't. Care." he said. His voice sounded like a groan.

Charlie stood up, walking at Justin. Justin backed away.

"Charlie," Justin said. "Are you in there?"

Justin took out the lighter and flicked it on. Charlie's eyes focused on it. Charlie reached out one hand to it. Then he grabbed the doorknob instead.

"Don't. Care." he repeated. That same dead voice. Zombie-Charlie slowly shut the door in Justin's face. He didn't even bother to slam it.

CHAPTER EIGHT
How to Save a Zombie

Chloe couldn't sleep that night. Poor Justin. How could he sleep with his zombie brother next door? And his dad didn't think anything seemed wrong!

CS — You guys up?

MB — Yes

Justin didn't answer.

CS — You scared?

MB — I have the frog

JG — Yes

Justin replied at last. Maybe to

both questions.

Chloe looked out her window. From here, she couldn't see anything wrong at Zephyr Terminal. It looked as empty as ever.

The green light she'd seen before flashed on. It blinked off just as fast.

CS Green light at Zephyr

CS The zombies?

But the zombies were already here. There shouldn't be a warning light.

Unless there was more than one train out there, waiting to come in. The stories about ghost train whistles in Bridgeside had been around for years. Just because they'd somehow let a train through didn't mean it was the only train.

CS A dispatch room controls a lot of trains, right?? We flipped the switch. We should flip it back. And maybe flip some other switches. Nothing's worse than zombies, right?

MB

MB Come plan at my house

MB Tomorrow

Chloe was able to sleep after that.

She was still tired when she reached Malik's house in the morning. Mrs. Bey let Chloe in. She looked sleepy, too.

"The boys are in the basement," Mrs. Bey said. "Putting together a puzzle, they said!"

Chloe found the boys waiting down in the dark, concrete basement.

Justin looked like he hadn't slept. "I bought that book online."

"What book?" Chloe asked.

"*Real Zombies*. The preview said something about salt. Turns out—salt's a cure for zombies. You have to make them swallow it. If they're still alive—"

"Slow down," Chloe said. "A zombie can be alive?"

Justin held up paper covered in notes.

"When someone alive is turned into a zombie, it's a trance," he said. "Like…hypnosis. They're mindless. Under magic control. They don't eat, don't sleep—"

Chloe frowned. "But if you're alive, and you don't eat—"

"You don't stay alive long," Justin said. "Salt is supposed to make zombies remember who they really are. Fire reminds them of being alive. But salt breaks the trance."

"That's weird," Chloe said.

"Everything's weird," Justin said. "This is our best shot. The oldest zombie story I found."

Malik held up his frog.

"I called the Bridgeside Pet Shop," he said. "They have five more frogs."

"Frogs, check," Chloe said. "What about firewood?"

"We're starting a fire?" Malik asked.

Justin pointed to a basement corner. Chloe and Malik looked. There was a huge stack of newspapers.

"What we really need," Justin said, "is a wagon."

"Like a little red wagon?" Malik said. He didn't have one, but his cousins did. They went over to his cousins' garage and then filled up the wagon. They got the rock salt their parents used to melt winter ice. They bought frogs. They crumpled up newspapers. They carried a squirt gun with salt water and a partly broken hockey stick.

It was high noon. And they were going to fight zombies.

This was the coolest day of Chloe's life so far. Just hopefully not her last day.

CHAPTER NINE
Plan of Action

They tugged the wagon under the fence. Justin took the box of frogs. Malik handed over his frog buddy, too.

"Stick to the plan," Chloe said. "It's a great plan."

Malik didn't think so. It was just their only plan.

Justin reached out and touched both their shoulders. Then he ran for the unlocked door.

Once Justin—and the frogs—were inside, the zombies started coming out of the tunnel. There were more new "living zombies" now. Staggering, moaning. Wearing grocery store uniforms.

Chloe lifted the rock salt bag out of the wagon. It was almost as big as her. Then she dropped it. She took the hockey stick. Malik took the squirt gun. Only newspapers stayed in the wagon.

"Now," she said. She scooped a handful of the chunky salt.

Malik held the lighter against the newspaper. It wouldn't burn long, not like wood. But the paper caught bright fire, fast. They had a wagon of fire.

← lit!

Malik pulled it, running. The living zombies came right after the fire.

The dead zombies didn't move away from the fire. But they didn't come after him, either.

Again, the zombie train chugged forward, out of the tunnel. A zombie in a driver's hat leaned out the front window. Chloe hit its hat off with a chunk of salt.

She used the hockey stick to shoot pieces of rock salt,

too. If they came close, she jabbed with the stick's broken end.

The train chugged toward her. More zombies jumped off it every minute. Chloe tried to keep them by the tracks.

Malik, watching, missed one zombie in a grocery store uniform coming close. Before she tackled him, he pulled out the tiny squirt gun. He shot salt water right in the zombie's open mouth.

She collapsed to the ground. He wondered if that was good or bad. He kept running with his wagon. The newspaper fire was already dimming.

Malik finally saw a zombie on the train watching the fire. Wearing normal clothes. Looking pretty alive still.

Charlie.

"Hey, Charlie Gill," Malik shouted. "I have your lighter!"

Zombie-Charlie didn't react. Malik didn't know much about Charlie, but…

Charlie really hadn't liked Chloe calling him

an idiot.

"How dumb are you, Charlie!" Malik shouted. "So stupid! Justin tried to tell you! You idiot!"

Charlie moaned and hopped off the slow-moving train. Jerkily, he came toward Malik.

Malik raised his squirt gun. Justin really needed to get to the dispatch room.

CHAPTER TEN
The Witch

Zephyr Terminal was empty again. Justin didn't know if the zombies were hiding from the frogs or if they were all outside.

He made it upstairs, no problem.

One zombie stood guard at the dispatch room's door.

It was the first zombie they'd seen. His cheekbone stuck out. His mouth hung open. No cure would help this guy. Had he just hopped a train one day, years ago, and been zombified?

Justin held his frog box out like a shield as he approached. The zombie shook, but it didn't leave. Justin threw a bag of salt from his pocket in the zombie's face.

It shrieked. So loudly Justin wanted to grab his ears. It backed up. Braced itself in the door.

Justin eyed the zombie's loose arm. He set down the box of frogs.

Then he reached out, grabbed the zombie's arm, and pulled hard. The arm came right off.

The zombie tried to lean forward and bite Justin. It tried to grab him with its remaining arm.

Justin opened the frog box and let them loose. Right on the zombie's feet. The zombie stumbled away. Far enough for Justin to get in the room and shut the door.

Watching the squiggly routes on the board, he tried every switch he could. Nothing. Then, one very rusty switch clicked. A new train route on the board lit up in red.

He turned the same dial as yesterday.

On the board, the red light moved toward the terminal.

From outside, he heard a train whistle. Not the zombie train. A second one.

The radio crackled. "Who's that?" a woman's voice snarled. "Who's in dispatch?"

Justin looked for a microphone. He didn't see one.

"Are you the witch?" he asked. "You're behind the zombies?"

"Is that a *child*?" the voice said. She laughed. "I'm behind everything. And I'm coming over to your side. No little child can stop me."

"Hey!" Justin said. "I'm eleven."

Then he turned the dial, hard, the other way.

Flipping the switch back.

GHAPTER ELEVEN
The Z Team

Chloe was keeping as many zombies on the tracks as she could. Then the green warning light flashed through the terminal window. She dashed away.

A train appeared near the river. A different one. A sleek black steam engine. It chugged right onto the broken tracks.

It slammed over all the zombies standing there. It smashed them into flying pieces of zombie limbs and clothes. These crumbled into gray-green dust as they hit the ground. The new train then slammed right into the zombie train, crumpling it more.

Three shadowy shapes—moving way too

fast to be zombies—jumped off the new train. Or maybe Chloe was seeing things. She blinked. Nothing but zombie dust.

The living Bridgeside zombies stared, mouths open. Malik used the chance to spray salt water into the mouths of all the zombies left. Charlie last.

Charlie fell over the second the salt hit his tongue. He joined deliveryman zombie and the others on the ground. They looked like they were sleeping, peacefully.

The new train had barely braked. But it started chugging backwards. As if being pulled. The zombie train, and any zombies still on board, went right behind it.

Justin had turned the dial back.

The trains sped back toward the river and disappeared.

Chloe went to Malik and looked down at the sleeping local "zombies."

Delivery guy moved. He climbed to his feet, eyes closed. The others followed. One by one, eyes shut. They walked away without staggering. Like they knew where to go.

Justin came running out of the terminal. He was holding—

"Is that an arm?" Chloe asked. It crumbled into dust when he tried to hand it over.

"You got the salt in Charlie?" Justin asked Malik.

"Yeah! And you got rid of the trains!" Malik said back.

Charlie and the others walked over the broken-down fence.

"Where are they going?" Chloe asked.

"I guess where legends say zombies go when they're cured," Justin said. "Home."

He was right. They followed Charlie straight home. Charlie laid down in his bed, eyes still closed. Then he woke up.

"Why are you in my room, nerd boy?" Charlie asked. "What's with your geek friends?"

"Actually, I'm a film buff," Malik said. "But who decided being a nerd, or a geek, was bad? We just care about stuff."

Charlie rubbed his eyes, confused. He looked more confused when Justin hugged him.

"You're okay? You don't remember

anything?" Justin asked.

"Remember what?" Charlie asked.

"Nightmares, I guess?" Justin said. "You were…groaning."

"I'm fine," Charlie said. "But thanks. For checking. Caring. Whatever. Now can you leave?"

Once out, the three high-fived and walked downstairs. Justin's dad was making lunch.

"Have you seen the salt?" Mr. Gill asked.

They tried not to laugh too hard.

Late at night, Chloe looked out her window. She sent a text:

CS Terminal's dark.

JG No train whistles either. I'll keep listening.

JG No more trains can come through right? Bridgeside's safe?

CS Of course it's safe. It's got us!

JG The Z Team

Chloe looked at her group message name—*Zephyr Team Project*. She deleted a few letters.

Falling asleep, she remembered the shadows from the second train. She'd fill Malik and Justin in later. The Z Team could tackle that tomorrow.

Inside Zephyr Terminal, three shadowy figures met under the clock.

"It's been a long time since we've been on this side, my friends," one said.

He smiled, with teeth white as the moon. And sharp as knives.

"Now. Who's thirsty?"

Want to Keep Reading?

Turn the page for a sneak peek
at the next book in the series.

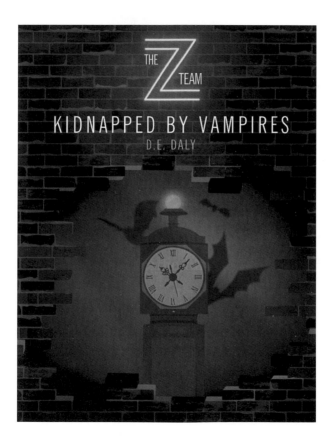

ISBN: 9781538381892

CHAPTER ONE
The Terminal Opens

Zephyr Terminal stayed dark. Chloe checked from her window every night.

Just weeks ago, Chloe and her friends had snuck into the closed train station. They had tracked spooky sounds. A strange green light. In the terminal's dispatch room, they'd turned a dial. A not-so-ghostly train showed up. Bringing a bunch of zombies to Bridgeside.

Chloe, Malik, and Justin sent the train back. All on their own. They'd decided to call themselves the Z Team. Ready for whatever came next.

But nothing else happened. Except

September arrived. School. Homework.

The adventure might be over.

Chloe went to school bored as usual. Then in the hall—she saw it. A flyer, showing the terminal.

Colony Tours, it read. *New! See inside Zephyr Terminal! Learn history!*

Chloe grabbed the flyer off the wall. In homeroom, she showed her friends.

Justin loved history. He'd never heard of the company.

"Maybe they're from out of town," Justin said.

"We have to investigate," Chloe said. "The very first tour! Let's do it."

"We have homework," Malik said. "The tours are at night. My parents work then."

"My older sisters will take us!" Chloe said. "El loves any excuse to take the car."

Chloe reminded the boys: when they'd sent the zombies back by train…she'd seen three shadowy shapes jump off. Everything might be quiet, dark. But now this. Something was up.

ABOUT THE AUTHOR

D.E. Daly can sometimes be found in her hometown of East Aurora, New York, a village full of haunted history and old railroad tracks. She studied writing in New Orleans and drifts back there once in a while for more of the city's magic and music. She is always chasing her next story—except the times when the story chases her.

THE **Z** TEAM

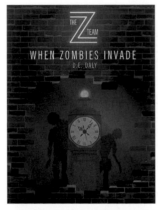

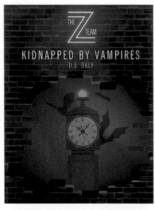

Check out more books at:
www.west44books.com

An imprint of Enslow Publishing

WEST **44** BOOKS™